T0370525

The High School Girl

The High School Girl

Education Transformation

TARA LOUISE

Library of Congress Control Number: 2017902164
ISBN: Hardcover 978-1-5245-2260-5
Softcover 978-1-5245-2259-9
eBook 978-1-5245-2258-2

Print information available on the last page.

Rev. date: 02/09/2017

To order additional copies of this book, contact:
Xlibris
1-800-455-039
www.Xlibris.com.au
Orders@Xlibris.com.au
753312

Contents

Acknowledgement

I originally wrote this book as an escape from the real world. There was always something exciting about writing a fiction novel that could twist and turn as rapidly as life. Unlike the real world, you can change the ending. As much as I wanted to finally be here and get published, I kept waiting; life kept getting in the way.

I cannot thank my friends enough for giving me that push to pursue what I wanted to do with my writing. My high school classmates, friends, family, and now even my work colleagues have been above and beyond supportive of my decision to pursue this.

Thank you to the hard-working team that have come together to publish this book.

CHAPTER 1

The Welcome

Hi, I am Onyx, and this is my story of grade 12. It's hard, but it's my story. It's the end of the holidays, and the new year has started. School is back with your usual students at high school.

'Hey, hey, hey! Welcome back, everyone, to Franklin High. The music is loud, and everyone is back. Cheerleaders, jocks, drama, and science—you name it. That's high school. Enjoy the next tunes that I dish out for you. This is your radio girl Heidi speaking. Have a fun-tastic first day back, and enjoy your High School Radio!'

'Oh my god, Hannah, have you checked out the new football jocks? Like, wow, they are so cheerleader boyfriend material. Girl, like, come on, we need to get a taste.'

'Stop. Handle yourself, Marsha. We cheerleaders do not go that easily. The jocks have to come to us, not the other way around. Got it?'

'Yeah, I know, girl, but they are fine. Oh! Who is that little cutie there?' asks Marsha.

'Oh, him. He must be Jason, the new jock to the team,' replies Hannah.

'Now he fine, girl—brown locks, the right height, a bit of muscle. Oh, did you see that he got class, girl? I got to get that!'

'Marsha, no! As next in line after me, you have to get the guys to come to you. Now come, we have to get some nerds to do our new year assignments,' snaps Hannah.

'Girl, you're right!'

'Did you see that? Cheerleader alert! And aren't they looking finer than usual, Jason?'

'Yeah, I . . . I . . . I guess so, man, but hey, do we always have to date the cheers of the school? Brian, Brian, are you listening?'

'Yeah, man, I'm sorry, but you have to learn cheerleaders are the best to get something on, if you know what I mean. Just hang with us, and you'll know the school soon enough, 'cause we are the jocks of this school. We own it.'

'Yeah, whatever,' mumbles Jason.

The school bell rings, and everyone starts to head into class. Over in the principal's office, I, a new student, am talking to her.

'Hi, and welcome to Franklin High, Miss . . . Miss Limestone. I hope you enjoy the year and stay with us until the year ends. Here is your timetable, and I hope you make some great new friends here at Franklin High.'

'Thanks, Miss . . . uh . . . Principal Glosten. I'm sure I will stay.'

'Yes, and I have seen your records. I will be keeping an eye on you. Setting fire to a school cafeteria and being suspended twenty-three times in year 11—well, this will not be accepted here at Franklin High. Now the other students and teachers will be waiting for you to join them, so off you go to Form. Enjoy your stay, Miss Limestone.'

'Yep, okay, form room, C2. Great. Bye, Principal Glosten.'

I walk out of her office and down the hall, looking for the right classroom.

'C2, C2, C2 . . . no. F1, D3 . . . ah, here we go, C2.'

Fantastic. A new school and new everything. At least there is no uniform. I enter the room, the door slammed shut behind me, and the useless babble comes to a sudden stop, with eyes staring at me, the newcomer.

'Ah, you must be Miss Limestone. Welcome to Franklin High. We have an extra-long form today for extra notices. I'm Miss Gardner. Now do tell us a bit about yourself.'

While I'm talking 'a bit about myself', whispers and mutters goes around the room, and unfortunately, I can hear every word.

'Hi, my name is Onyx.'

'What's with her hair?'

'I just moved here from Transylvania in Louisiana and have settled here in Salem for the last three weeks.'

'Witch.'

'And I guess that's all I *wish* to say. Can I sit down now, Miss Garner?'

'Yes, yes, of course, uh, Onyx. Take a seat anywhere you want.'

I walk up between the desks to the back corner and sits quickly down where a shadow sort of covers me, though not by much.

'Damn, Hannah, did you see that long almost-black hair? Baggy pants, long down-to-your-ankles black jacket, and a vest . . . I have seen that shirt. It has one thick strap that hangs on her arm, not on her shoulder, like the other strap. And look at that bag! What is with the black hessian satchel? But what's with leather necklace? It looks like a collar. Girl, she is going to have fun here at Franklin High.'

'Students, I just have to see the principal. Be nice to Onyx, all right?' Announced Miss Gardner.

'Yes, I saw that Marsha, and wow, long hair on a girl like that! Come on, she looks like a Goth. She is not going to get a single boyfriend.'

'Hannah, wasn't it? Well, for your information, I am not one who waits around for a guy to notice me. That's why I don't follow a certain group like you, and Marsha follows you around and tries to fit in 'cause she wants to be popular or be waited upon. But life is all about being yourself. Have you have heard of the word *individuality*? It's not just following school tradition or your mates, because each person is different. Now I think I have made myself clear and, unfortunately, noticed.'

'Dude, did you see that now? That Onyx chick is going to get it. No one talks to the cheer captain like that.'

'Shh, Brian, this is one girl I wanna hear out.'

'Jason, is your head on straight? We go for cheerleaders, not newbies, well, unless they're cheerleaders—top, action-packed cheerleaders.' Protested Brian.

'Oh, look who said some babble—Onyx the Limestone. We follow cheer history, and I bet you can't cheer like us.' Challenged Hannah.

'Not cheer on the dance side, but I could cheer chants better.' Replied Onyx.

'Oh, bring it, newbie.'

'Oh, I will!'

The battle begins. Hannah stands up and starts off with the Franklin High cheer. I sit still in my seat, wondering what stupid things she would do.

'When we go and do our cheer, you'll be coming to us, dear. We don't care about the rest. You all know Franklin High's the best.'

'Oh, look! Oh, wow, you think you're cool! What you don't get, with those moves, you look like a fool.'

'I am sassy. I am classy. These moves I do are called cheers. I'm the head. I'm good in bed. Oh, look, I'm your worst fear.' Cheered Hannah.

The cheering rises for Hannah, and she smiles and thinks she has won.

'Ha, unimpressive! Try this, cheerleader. Beware, I'm the cat, and you are a rat. Your cheering is so poor. Now watch out for my claw.'

'A cat for you and me a rat. Look in the mirror, Goth. Check out your mouth, it got froth.'

I stand up to finish this. 'Blonde hair, blue eyes, there is no surprise. You think when you shake it, you got the prize. Wake up, cheerleader. With a skirt that short, you must be a queer leader—not to mention you spend a lot time with a lot of girls.'

'Garr, well, newbie, try this while cheering. It's known as dancing. Look where to there is where I am. I—ah!'

Unfortunately, for Hannah, she trips over a chair and makes a drastic fall to the ground, landing on her ass and losing the 'bring it on' cheer battle. Without laughing, I stop what I've been doing and quickly sit back down.

I heard something and, unfortunately, warn the cheerleader, 'You better get up, loser. The teacher is here.'

'Liar, you are nothing but a newbie, fake—eh!'

'What is this, Hannah? Do you not like the new person in our class?' asked Miss Gardener.

'No, Miss, I don't!'

'Well, too bad. She stays.'

The bell rings, and all the students go to their next class. I have a hard time in my first two classes. English with Hannah—wow, how fun for me. Oh well, I've taken that well, creating a news article for one of our assignments in the coming weeks. Studies of Society and Environment (SOSE for short) is full of forest stuff. Finally, lunch comes around, and all I want to do is take a walk around the school to find a place of my own.

Thank the powers to be, that I don't have to go into class for another hour and a half. Then I have Hannah,

Marsha, Jason, and Brian in science. Golly, what a first day. Soon I can go home for the day. Oh, well.

During my walk, I see the funniest thing; groups of certain people are all together. I walk down the hall past the gymnasium, where all the cheerleaders are eating salads and whatever fits their certain diet. In the workout gym, most of the jocks are in there, feeding on protein bars and fighting over who is stronger and who can have what exercise machine for what.

Further around the corner are the science laboratories with all your humble science people trying to see if they mix that with this, they can make a chemical reaction. I have to stop a couple of corners around to see what the high-pitched screaming is all about, but it is the drama club doing what they do—acting to be on Broadway— but as if, it is very challenging to get onto Broadway. They need to be aiming lower to get higher. Oh well, what you are you going to do. I don't want to stand in the way of peoples' dreams, no matter how foolish they seem.

Back in the gymnasium, the cheerleaders are all talking about Onyx, the newcomer.

'Girl, come on, please tell me you have seen the girl. Like, no girl wears her hair like that here in Salem. Am I right or what, girls?'

'Hmm, you are right, like the dance that I was so humiliated in, she knew her words, garr. I need to know more about her.'

'Why?' ask the other cheerleaders.

'Because nobody comes into my school or my class without me knowing everything I can about them. Here is a little cheer for you to get the picture. Give me an *O*. Give me an *N*. Give me a *Y*. And give me an *X*. What does that spell? *Onyx*. She, she, she came into my school, but she has to learn she goes by my rule. There is a secret, I know, deep in there. I need to know so I can make it fair. Why, why, why? It doesn't make sense. She is strange and always so tense. I'm gonna know her now with you, if it's the last thing this cheer captain's gonna do.'

'Wow, girl, calm down. Thank God that it's only me and you and the cheerleaders here, or you would be, like, a loser.'

'Hmm, yeah, you're right. Come on, let's go to Brian. You hear, we are still going out. Oh, star quarterback, brown locks—oh, he is dreamy, right?'

'Girl, you are back in the zone. Why not?'

'Hey, girls! Hey, babe, can I have some?' Smiled Brian.

'Sure, go for it.'

'Girl, I need a boyfriend.' Muttered Marsha.

'Mmmwa. Sorry. Oh yeah, boyfriend, yeah. Why don't you go with Jason? Wait, where is he?' Questioned Hannah.

'Babe, I don't know. He didn't come with us here. Mmwa.'Replied Brian.

'Hmmm, well, we are going to find him. You keep up the best you can, honey.'

'Come on, girl, let's find my boyfriend-to-be.'

I have walked all around this school. Sitting here outside won't do much. There has to be a place where I can sit on my own. Oh great, the jock.

'Hey, I heard what you had to say in class this morning, and I agree with you. People have a right to be their own thing.'

'Oh, that's odd coming from a jock.'

'Well, that's because I met Brian when I was playing football. I just transferred from Los Angles, and I was starting this year here in Salem. Brian went strange on me with all this "You are so good. We need another mate to join. Come on, be a jock." But in Los Angles, we were our own person. No one judged you by the groups that you hung with, and that is really difficult here.' He sighs and looks down. 'I guess you and me are a bit the same.' He looks up. 'Hey, where did she go? I have to find her.'

CHAPTER 2

Who Is Onyx Limestone?

Jason runs all around the school, trying to find me, but what he doesn't realise is that I am watching him the whole time. What I don't know is that when I stop for a break, standing and watching the sights of the town in front of me and drinking my milk, someone close by is talking.

'H-how did she get up there?' Asked Hannah.

'Girl, she probably took the stairs and climbed out a window.' Replied Marsha.

'No, there are no stairs that go high enough. There has to be some other way she got up there. It's the south wall. No one can get there.'

'Get over it, girl.'

'No!' Screamed Hannah.

'Huh?' I tilt my head to the left and witnessed a shocked, stunned, and angry look on Hannah's face. With a salute her way, I jump down the opposite side to her and Marsha. I wish I could be in two places at once just to see the look on her face.

'Garr, come on, we need to find out more.'

'No, girl, I am going to cheer. Come on, get your mind off this Onyx girl.'

'Mmm . . . I guess. Maybe Brian can sizzle me.'

Hannah and Marsha leave, but just around the corner, Jason overheard the whole story.

'So she is something different altogether.'

After I jump off the side of the building, I quickly made my way to the north tower. I don't know what to do completely. I either use this to my advantage or hide it for a while. For the last hour of break, I sit in the shadows on top of the north tower. Because of my black clothes, no one notices me. I don't think anyone can see me as they will have to be above me to spot me. After a while, I drift off into a doze. I'm awakened by the radio girl Heidi.

'Hey, that was another funky song by Simple Plan. Next song I'll be bringing you are "Shut Up and Drive" by Rihanna. "Lithium" is the awesome song next by Evanescence. Well, you have seen the newcomers to Franklin High. Oh well, the more the better, I suppose. Now here we have been given the privilege of the head cheerleader, Hannah ha, ha, ha . . . Here you go, cheer captain. This is her review of one of the new students . . . Onyx!

'Huh, she is going to talk to everyone about me, gar. I can't let this happen.'

There's a clearing with no one around. About three jumps, and I will be off the high tower.

'Well, thank you, Heidi. Okay, well, we have all seen her around. Maybe you know the outfit and all. Well, I saw her—oh, look, she is here outside the radio studio! Come have a good look at the new student Onyx and get a load of her.'

Hmm. With a smile on my face, I decide to walk towards her. Hannah, looking a bit scared, stands her ground.

'Come on in, Onyx, and let's hear a bit about you.'

I'm close enough to say what I need to say, but I want to stick it. I open the door, go right up to Hannah, and say, 'Listen, I don't do the new-student traditions. Now get off my back or get a face rearrangement, you Can't-Understand-Now-Tata. Figure that out, but don't have a headache about it.'

I walked out, with Hannah about to blow off frustration.

'Onyx, you garr, I will get back at you!'

'Okay, well, that was Onyx and Hannah. Now we have Evanescence's "Lithium". Be free, everyone! I'm Heidi, your high school radio DJ, saying, "Have a good next lesson!"'

Half an hour before I am in another strange class. I'm thinking, why is it that because I am different, people just assume I need to be exiled from the rest? Why is it that wherever I go, I cannot say the truth to anyone? I guess that's why I liked Transylvania. If it wasn't for the secret science organisation known as the SOMMIT chasing me, the cafeteria would not have had to be destroyed. But no. Tests, tests, and tests—that's all they ever think of doing.

Well, I guess because of how I am, that's why they want me and why they killed my parents.

'Hey, I'm glad I found you. Uh . . . why are you sitting in a tree? Oh well, can you come down please?'

'What if it is comfortable up here? Can't you talk to me if I am on the low branch near you?'

'Yeah, that's fine. I just want to talk to you.'

'Okay, here I am. What do you wish to talk about?'

'Wow, how did you do that so fast? Ahem, well, anyway . . . So far, you seem to be the only person I can relate to 'cause, well, we are both individuals and we like to stay that way. We have to show the school who we really are, right, Onyx?'

'No, I wish to be seen but not heard—that is the way of me. I have never opened myself up to show my true colours, if that is what you're saying.'

'Why not?'

'Because I am too different and people will not understand me.'

'But you can at least try, and it . . . it won't go past my ears. I can completely understand people that are different. Let's just say it's in my family.'

What am I supposed to say to him—that if I could, I would but I'd end up like in Transylvania? The school bell rings. Yes, thank you, bell. Oh no, I am in his class. Damn.

'I have to get to class.'

'Hey, Onyx, wait up. We . . . we are in the same class. Can I walk you there?'

'No! Buzz off, okay? You are a jock. Go admire the cheerleaders.'

'I'm only a jock on the outside, and you know that!'

In science, we take down notes on physics and then have a quick revision practical on Newton's law. Jason tries to be paired up with me, but Marsha wants him, so that's good. The class doesn't have enough to make even pairs, so I'm left on my own, just the way I like it—well, just the way I am used to. It is a long class, but I manage to get through it.

'Hey, Onyx, I don't think you get this, but here at Franklin High, the head cheerleader is supposed to know everything about every student, so you better spill soon so I can know you because, well, I am the head cheerleader. Ha ha, ha ha. See ya, loser!'

'Oh, Hannah, don't worry yourself. You have seen enough of me to know I have surprises up my sleeves. Laterz!'

Yes, it's the end of school. Finally, I can go . . . home, I guess.

'Hey, Onyx, is that you? It's me, Sinca.'

'Oh, hey, Sinca! How was your first day of year 4?'

'Oh, it was good. I met this girl, and she is really nice. What about you, Onyx?'

'Oh, uh . . . it was fun. Met lots of people. Sinca, I am going to take the long way . . . home. Tell Aunt Jo that I will be in late, 'kay?'

'Sure, Onyx, anything for you.'

'Thanks. Bye, Sinca.'

'Bye, Onyx.'

She runs off, while I take a detour through the streets and lanes.

'Finally, this city can have someone new looking after them.'

I take a nice long journey along the rooftops, watching and looking at everything I can. I'm guessing by now you have figured out that I have cat or feline abilities, whichever translation takes your fancy. Well, please do keep it a secret.

While I'm sitting up, catching some sun on a rooftop, I sense something familiar in the town. When I look over to check it out, I'm shocked. It's two scientists that I'm very well known to. They are the reason the cafeteria was burnt down.

These scientists really have been trying all their lives to find something cool, and they see me—the cat eyes, collar, abilities—and now they want to run tests. But how did they find me so quickly? Well, I don't know, but I can't hang around the rooftops any more, or they will find me for sure.

It's not like I have anywhere to go. I am an orphan. My mother died after birth because of a scientist. To help you understand, I'll try to look back at my memories. My mother was like me—with the feline abilities. But my father would not accept me for my abilities even though he seemed to love my mother. However, he too was killed by the SOMMIT. I managed to hide and become unnoticed by the SOMMIT until later on. That was when I first met them officially. I have been hidden and raised by a gun expert who had originally told the SOMMIT about my mother.

He told me the truth when I was fourteen. Now for the last few years, the SOMMIT has tried dangerously to capture me but never succeeded.

I guess Aunt Jo is my mother figure now. She accepts me, sort of. Well, I will have to find out how the SOMMIT found me. Night comes, and night goes. Not much happens when you clean, eat, and sleep in a house full of orphans. But I suppose I can't complain. It is the last place the SOMMIT will look for me. I still wonder why they are here. Maybe they're looking for some other creature. Are there really that many of us left?

'Onyx! Hey, Onyx!'

'Oh, great, I'm at school. What is it, Jason?'

'I want, uh—'

'Oh, Jason, come drop that loser newbie for me 'coz I'm a sizzling girl in your view.' Interrupted Marsha.

'Just go, Jason. I don't need you.'

Yes, thank you, Marsha, for saving the day without any comment.

'Oh yeah, Onyx, what is with that? Do y'all see? This is how ya do it, cheerleader. Check it out, yeah. And you got what, a long black skirt and a vest? Your hair is still down, and you have that jacket that goes to your heels. You are messed up, yo.'

'Marsha, leave her alone.' Said Jason.

'What you sticking up for this newbie for? She isn't natural. Hey, hey, hey, hey, don't you walk away from me! What you doing? Come back here. Oh, you lucky newbie.'

Okay, that's very bizarre. Marsha needs to learn proper words. I guess I spoke to soon about her not saying any comments. Oh well, looks as if I have to go to my homeroom. Not much is happening today—maths, manual arts, computer studies, and that is it. Thank God. The bonus about senior years is that all you have to complete is the bare minimum.

'Well, look who it is, the girl who thinks she can take over this school that is all mine.'

'Girl, you said it. You better make way for the queen bee. She rules this school.'

'Ha ha ha, I thought it was the footballers with no brains, but I see there is room for the cheerleaders under the—'

'All right, class, sit down and quiet down! I want you to be silent for the entire time you are here. Someone last night thought it was funny to graffiti our room in C block. So no one is to log on to the computers, or they will serve detention with me.'

Yeah, like anyone listens to her. Almost everyone hops on the computer. That's when I see something very odd on Hannah's computer. It's an ad from the SOMMIT (Science of Military, Magical, Interesting Things). It reads, '*We from the SOMMIT are looking for something that has recently gotten away from us, a young seventeen-year-old student known as Onyx. She is a suspicious character, so if you see her, contact this number immediately: 55682142. Do not do anything. She can be a handful. Just contact the SOMMIT.*

So that's how they found me. Someone has contacted the SOMMIT, but who? The bell sounded, and I hear a funny comment as we leave the classroom.

'Hey, Onyx, did you see that ad that I saved? "You can be quite a handful". Yeah, right. Anyway, at least it will get you out of this town.'

'Hannah, what is your problem with me? Is it because I upstaged you yesterday and made you look like a total fool? You must tell me what you said to the SOMMIT!'

'Why would I tell you anything? It is obvious that they want you, so why is it that they want you, hmmm?'

'I can't say. Just please tell me what you told them.'

'See ya later, Onyx. Ha ha ha ha!'

'I know that they are here in town, but do they know I go to Franklin High?'

'Wow, don't you sound desperate and upset! Well, if you must know . . .'

'Mm?'

'Then I won't tell you! He he, ha ha, I am so brilliant. You obviously have to watch your step. Later, Onyx.'

Oh no, she has said something, and I have to find out what, or I may be in big trouble. Oh, she's right. I *am* upset. I have not shed a tear since I was little. Oh well, one tear is nothing. I have to get out of here, but what can I do? I am safer here than anywhere else in this small town.

Math is full of numerals. They say I'm smart and have potential in that class. I giggle to myself slightly; they will probably select me for the stupid mathletes. Well, I guess that's what happens when you are too busy looking over your shoulder all the time. You get distracted and look smart.

Manual arts is a bore, absolute bore because no one can be bothered to do anything except for half a dozen people. The girls are mingling, and the boys are being boys, lighting plastic on fire and seeing who can go out with whom in our class. The seventy-minute class went by very slowly. I managed to make what is starting to look like a car out of wood. Then we go back on the computers for my ITC class. For those who don't know, ITC is about computer skills, and that is definitely the most boring class. With no login, I have to use another student's login.

The class goes by faster than expected, and I'm able to leave. I catch up with Sinca and ignore the comments from Hannah and Marsha. At the orphanage, I do the dishes then babysit the younger kids as they play with Lego on the roof's balcony. Don't be alarmed. I watch them closely, and no one tries to climb the wall, but what I do watch out for most of all is the SOMMIT.

'Onyx! Onyx? Onyx!'

'Huh? Oh, sorry, Sinca. What's the matter?'

'Well, Aunt Jo wants to see you.'

'Okay, but what about the children?'

'She said I could take care of them.'

'Ok, thank you.'

I walk down the stairs and meet up with Aunt Jo.

'Onyx, I noticed you were doing some extra jobs around the house, and I understand that you have had a rough past and don't wish to speak about anything. But in the last three weeks that you have been here, this is the day that you have helped out the most. The children love you, and I want to know if you are all right.'

'Yes, Aunt Jo, it is just different settling into a new school.'

'Ah yes, well, don't worry about it too much. Now I'll give you the rest of the evening off. Just go do what you need to do . . . maybe prepare for your uncles' visit tomorrow.'

'What uncles? I have no family left.'

'Oh well, a schoolgirl came by, asking if anyone knew you. I said I did. Then she continued on about two scientists from . . . I think it was SOMMIT, a special organisation of something or other. She said that they were your uncles.'

'No! Do you know—ugh, they killed my parents and are after me. Who said this to you?'

'I think she said her name was Hannah. We bumped into each other by the market, and I'm sure they are not after you if they are your family.'

'They are *not* my family!'

'Well, don't worry about it, dear. I'm sure they'll lose the address or go down the wrong street. Just go upstairs and relax. I shall call you down for dinner. Then you shall go to bed. No exploring around tonight.'

CHAPTER 3

Science or Torture

What a way to get my heart racing. Aunt Josephine—or Aunt Jo, as we call her—is terrible at giving directions. That still doesn't make me feel any safer. I rest my worried head on to my soft pillow as I anxiously consider my options. I can just flee again, start over. But the SOMMIT probably have surveillance at every exit out of Salem. Maybe I can hide in the crowd for a little bit until I can figure out what to do. After a sleepless night, I make my way silently to school. The white-painted brick building for now is my sanctuary. The two towers representing the north and south hold proudly to the sky. How I wish I can just hide there until this nightmare calms down. I'm through the gates, and the bell sings endlessly in my ears. No other sounds seemed to enter. I'm utterly distracted on what's going to happen next. What will happen in the next chapter of my life?

Miss Gardener is head of the science department, so she's away, and we go straight into our first class, which is ITC.

'Okay, class. Now we have two guests coming to our school today. They are here from the Department of Science. They will be travelling around the school at lunch and are currently in our science laboratories in J block, giving a talk about what they do. We will all stand behind our chairs *after* we all complete the typing levels 1, 2, and 3 . . . Go,' said the teacher.

Fun, absolute fun. Scientists is all we need to see because everyone is just *so* worried about their future and what they want to do. Come on. What about me? What can I do but run away from the SOMMIT or everyone else who spreads the rumour of who I truly am. It makes me feel so weak. It's like I am in a constant loop. The world never changes. I run, hide, and repeat. I can't strive for things like everyone else. I just wish I'm a normal person. I have seen more in my life than anyone I know.

They say when you have undergone traumas, your brain may hide the details because they are too horrific. I sigh. Let's get these stupid levels 1, 2, 3 done. Yep, I am done. I'm the fifteenth person to finish in my class. In half an hour, everyone is finished, and we sit up, waiting to go to see these career-encouraging scientists.

'Class, slow down when you get outside the classroom.'

We walk along before organising back into our lines against the wall. That's when Hannah comes up to me with her sheep, Marsha.

'Oh, has that long black jacket come out of your *unfashionable* wardrobe? Hmm, let's see. You have tight black trousers and a navy-blue collared shirt. Yeah, girl, you never gonna fit in here.'

'That's true, Marsha, and she may not stick around that long.'

'Shouldn't you girls be in the classroom, waiting for your names to be marked off the roll?'

'Jason, you should not be ratting up the cheerleader groove.'

'Marsha, Hannah, go *now*!' Snapped Jason.

'Fine.'

'Fine.'

'Onyx, listen, you can't go into this classroom.'

'Why?'

'Trust me, Onyx. You have to stay away from this room. I can't say any more.'

He leaves quite quickly, and I wonder, but it doesn't bother me as I'm too steamed about Hannah and Marsha. The students have been given a talk about the equipment they will use and how to use them. It sounds interesting, huh. Maybe we can play musical beakers later. Well, we walk in and sit down. Jason is beside me, nervously twitching. Marsha is next to him, then Hannah, and her football jock, Brian.

It isn't until the teacher hits me to look up at the speakers that I notice. When I saw first look up at the desk, I freeze. I am pretty sure my heart has stopped, as does my breathing. I don't see scientific equipment; I see familiar weapons. That's when I could have leapt out of my chair. Do I run? Do I stay put?

There are two men in white laboratory coats; one is speaking to the other while he looks at all the faces in the room. He is a small man with blonde bushy hair—not a fashionable bushy, but more like he had not brushed it in days. Rectangular-shaped glasses sit low on his nose as he peers over them, scanning the room. The other is a taller man with neat brown hair. He is wearing round-shaped glasses that sit high on his nose. The reflection makes it impossible to see his eyes. Name tags sit straight on both their coats.

Shivers suddenly go down my spine like waves on the ocean. I'm eye to eye with the shorter man. Silently time seems to travel slowly as we both wait for the other to make a move. I leap from my seat, and the men grab their weapons, following me out. I run as fast as I can on the cream-tiled floor, knowing full well what their weapons can do. I need to get as much distance as possible. Long-range tranquilizer darts come shooting past me. Their weapons have become a lot more difficult than I thought they'd be. They yell at me to stop so I can go quietly in, but that don't work.

I shout back, 'Come and get me, and then you can have me!'

The weapons that they're using miss me. Other than tranquilizer darts, they are shooting small explosive devices. Every time they miss, they destroy a piece of the school. I cannot imagine the amount of trouble they would get into. They must have realised that, with my enhanced agility, their tactics would not work. In the time it takes them to change ammunition, I leap upstairs to catch my breath.

They follow me as per usual, but this time, they have a trick for me. Their weapons are as big as bazookas! Instead of shooting an explosive, it shoots out a grappling chain that snatches my right ankle as I leap from the landing. They tug back, sending me off balance, while the other weapon snatches my left wrist. I'm in trouble. I fall to the floor below with two limbs out of action. Luckily, cats land on their feet, I guess. The moment I land, they pull the chains tight and immobilise my left ankle.

'Now if you be a good little kitty cat, we won't shoot you,' says the blonde-haired man.

'What's going on, Onyx?' asks Jason.

'Has this abomination not told you about her? We shall shed some light on the mysterious ways of your new student Onyx. She is not like any ordinary teenage girl. The rumours of her burning down parts of her school are because we caused it, trying to get this half-cat, half-human abomination,' says the brown-haired man.

'Well, that explains everything,' says Jason.

'I thought there was something strange about you, Onyx, especially when I found you on the south tower roof,' says Hannah.

Gasps go over the crowd of students and teachers. They've followed the commotion out of curiosity and have been just in time to see me bound like an animal.

'Where are her parents?' asks the principal.

I shout to everyone the truth, 'Dead—thanks to them!'

Gasps go over the crowd once again.

'Well, we should introduce ourselves before we leave with our feral cat. My shorter colleague is Rohan, and I am John.'

'Shut up. Just shut up! You think because she has special abilities, you can treat her like an experiment? That is appalling! She is a human being, and I will stand up for her to show that we are not categorised, that we can be normal people, and that we don't have to run with the crowd and say what they say. We have a right to do and say what our heart and soul tell us we should say and do. They may not always be right, but it is our choice to make our mistakes and learn.' Protested Jason.

'Sorry you feel like that, mate, but no one seems to be supporting you there.'

'That's right, Rohan. You see, we have the firepower, and we have our stray, so we shall say goodbye. We have our prize and will be off.'

'You bastard!'

'Jason, no!'

'Onyx? But why? You have no reason to be treated this way.'

'No, I don't, but I'm not letting any more innocent blood be spilled because of these jerks.'

'But I can't just stand here.'

'Yes you can, and you must!'

'Onyx . . .'

'Let's go before I get bored and wish to get away, again!'

'All right, let's make this painful.' John laughed.

We walk out civilly. I could hear Jason protesting.

'How could all of you just stand there and watch a student be taken in front of our eyes? She is a human being, and you're just standing there, scared of what may happen.'

'Well, at least she is out of my school.' Stated Hannah.

'Yeah, girl, now that we have handed Onyx to the SOMMIT, we can get back to normal.'

'You did it, Hannah and Marsha.'

'What are you on about, sweetie?'

'Don't call me sweetie, Marsha.'

'Get over it, newbie jock!' Said Hannah.

'Shut up, shut up, all of you! Stop judging people by their categories. Everyone has a different personality, and I don't know about all of you, but I believe Onyx. I am going to save her.'

'Mr Hornatt, you are not allowed to leave school premises. Mr Hornatt!' Cried Principal Glosten.

'Now, now, kitty cat, you won't feel a thing until we are ready to test,' says Rohan.

'Yeah, like you can hold me in these stupid handcuffs.'

'Onyx, don't you get it? With this chemical, after it has been injected into your bloodstream, you shall fall off into a sleep long enough for us to get you to our lab.' John smiles.

'Catch me first.'

I run away down the hall, wiggling my hands out of the handcuffs and dropping them on the tiles.

'You got the gun aimed yet, Rohan?'

'Yes, I do.'

'Then fire!'

Sure enough, they fire the needle into the air, chasing my movements down the hall until I feel a point enter through my skin. Tingling waves crash through my body. This formula is quick, my legs give way, and I crash on to the tiles, sliding to a stop. I'm trying desperately to get up, but my body does not comply with my mind.

'Nice shot, Rohan! Now do you get it, kitty? You cannot win and get away from us, not this time.'

'Your mother was an extraordinary experiment but did not hold the potential of what you possess.' Said Rohan.

'You b-bastard, I shall stop your foul experiments on people that are different.'

'Hmm, looks like someone is tired. Why you don't sleep, kitty, or do you need warm milk?' Rohan laughs.

'Onyx!' screams Jason. 'You bastards, what did you do to her!'

'We put her into a catnap. Now back off, kid, or we will have to take harsh action.'

'Argh . . . uh, very well then.'

'Good boy, now step away from the girl, and we shall take her away.'

'Yes, sir,' grumbles Jason.

They took her away, and he watches them drive away in a white van. His stomach has a tingly feeling, and he knows that it means he's worried about what they'll do to Onyx. He signals a taxi and directs the driver to follow the van. I cannot lose Onyx to be tested like some animal. It's wrong and barbaric.

As they follow, his thoughts go to his family. What if they have met people in the SOMMIT? Are they scattered around like normal people? How will you identify one outside of a laboratory coat?

The chase leads him to a large warehouse, it's almost noon. He knows it may be hard to get inside, but he has to try. He just hopes Onyx is okay by the time he finds her.

Uh, I feel weak and horrible. Where am I? Oh, that's right, Rohan and John gave me a chemical to knock me out. Well, this has taken a turn for the worst, by the looks of things. Didn't think I would actually get caught. The weapons have become more advanced than I expected them to be.

'Oh, so you have awakened from your slumber,' says Rohan.

'Don't try to get out of those chains. You are well secure to do what we need to do.' John smiles.

'Argh, you can't hold me here like some animal, you cruel bastards!'

'I think you will find that we can. You aren't going anywhere, kitty.'

'You better back away before my claws come out, Rohan!'

'Okay then, we shall leave you until you have settled down and we are ready,' replied Rohan.

This is not good, not good at all. The chains are rustling, and it doesn't seem like I can slip out of them. I look around the warehouse; the steel walls have chains hanging for captives. There are tanks and operating tables around, as well as weapons stuck on the opposite corner. There are stairs going down, where the two scientists go, and stairs that go up to a small door.

The door starts to creek as it slowly opens. I'm surprised to see that it's Jason. What is he doing here? How did he find me? Why? I do not understand.

'Onyx, I am here to get you out of here.'

'Quiet down, you will make them come back.'

'Sorry, are you all right?'

'Yeah, I seem to be fine, but how did you get here?'

'I caught a cab and followed you here.'

'Fair enough. Now I believe that if you look over there on that table, you should be able to find a key to get me out of these old shackle things.'

'All right, I'll go look.'

'Hurry, I think they are coming.'

'What should I do?'

'Hide—what else?'

'Uh, right.'

'Do you think we should keep the eyes or sell the eyes, Rohan?'

'I recon study them then sell them, but I wish we can keep the kitty since she is quite beautiful.'

'Now, now, John . . . you know that last time we kept an experiment, the flame girl, she burnt half of your chest.'

'Don't remind me. That scar still hurts.'

'Okay, well, let's see if scat cat has settled down.'

'What exactly are you going to do to me?'

'Well, we have thought of numerous activities that we could do to find out why you are made like this, so we are going to do skin, blood, hair, and spit tests. After that, we were thinking of mating with you to see if you are more cat or human.'

'Gross! And how will mating with me help with the cat or human thing?'

'You see, both Rohan and I believe that if we can create more like you and figure out everything there is to know about you, we can start our new human race. The SOMMIT may not know of this, but it is fun on our part.'

'We already have sighted a mermaid in the Caribbean and a grizzly guy who is half polar bear, scaring the tourists in Greenland.'

'Not to mention a female descendant of the Loch Ness monster.'

'But I happen to be the only one you have caught.'

'Hmm, yes, but not for long.'

'Take this bastard!' Yelled Jason.

'That kid!'

'Our gun! Don't do it, kid!' shouted Rohan.

'Jason, those are the chain guns. Shoot them now!'

'Got it.'

It was like watching a play in a drama. The bad guys get caught in the end.

'I don't know about you, Jason, but I think these freaks should be hung up like an animal.'

'Yeah?'

'Why did you come after her?' asked Rohan.

'Because I care about her. Even if we haven't spoken much, I understand where she is coming from. I couldn't stand by, knowing that you could treat her inhumanely, when what she deserves is to be left alone.'

'Hey, Jason, now that you have them tied up, could you unlock me? Then I'll help you with the rest.'

'Sure, now where are the keys?'

I'm so surprised that someone whom I completely ignored would end up to be someone who would save me.

'Thanks, those shackles were quite annoying.'

'No problem. Now what's your idea?'

'I'll show you.'

CHAPTER 4

The Escape

I grab John and place his arms and legs in shackles then do the same to Rohan on the other side of the warehouse. My blood starts to boil. Burning into my memory are images scattered on a table of the SOMMIT 'dealing' with innocent creatures. There was what looked to be a nine-year-old girl with long pointy ears and small fairy wings coming out of her back. The image is of her screaming as they peeled part of her skin off her body. A young ten-year-old boy with long pointy ears and long fingernails was muzzled as they pierced a tag through his ear, like what farmers do to their cattle.

I scatter all the pictures across the table, and they land on the floor. My anger rises greatly from those photographs. Uncontrollably, I want nothing more than to see the SOMMIT burn. I lash out at the five tanks, destroying them. Ice-cold water rushed out over me and on to the floor. Jason tries to approach me. His reaction is timid and frightful as he sees my eyes, pure cat's eyes filled with rage, and my canine teeth have lengthened into fangs. By this time, the tables have been knocked over, and I cannot hear the sounds of Rohan and John shouting at me. Leaping down the stairs, I see utensils and explosive devices. Some different-coloured chemicals are also down there. I brush my arms through the shelves, knocking all the chemicals to the floor, smashing the glass bottles that hold them.

I grab a belt holding a hand grenade and hold it with my mouth. I run up the stairs on all fours. Quickly, I pull the pin off and throw it down the stairs I just came from. Finally, this warehouse is going to burn to the ground. I stand up on my two legs, starting to calm down from my rage. I run over to Jason, who is at the door he came through. We run up and jump off into the large garbage bin, and then we jump out, run towards the road, and turn around when we're clear of the explosion.

Jason is shaking, and his eyes are bulged. I watch and glare with an evil smile as the building blows up in flames, creating commotion in the other nearby warehouses. The warehouse doesn't fall to the ground, but it's burning as if the fire is dancing at its freedom. Jason grabs my hand, but I don't really notice at first. Then another explosion sets off, sending more dancing flames to the sky. Jason squeezes my hand and jumps; his whole body begins to shake.

'Onyx, I-I can understand the amount of pain and anger you have for these people, but letting them die like this will be murder for you. At least let them live please.'

'Fine, but they do deserve this fate.'

I run as fast as I can across the road and into the flames. The heat is tremendous, and the dancing flames are magical. I have no time to waste admiring my work.

I find John, who is covered in black ash and has been knocked unconscious from the lack of oxygen in the air. I jump over what used to be scaffolding and manage to get John out of harm's way. I turn around to go find Rohan. I see Jason coming up to see if John is alive. I go towards the direction of where I locked Rohan up, and I see that the chains have been snapped. I think that he might have gotten away until I see parts of a shredded white coat and a pair of shoes. He was underneath the metal plank. I lift the large piece of metal off Rohan then drag him out to where John and Jason are.

'Thanks, Onyx. I knew you could do it.'

'Yeah, yeah, just tell me, are they alive?'

'John's heartbeat has slowed down to a steady beat, and by the looks of Rohan, he has suffered an arm injury but is still alive.'

'Do you have a phone?'

'Yes, did you want me to ring the ambulance?'

'Yes, but first, save this number, okay?'

'Sure, fire away.'

'All right, 55682142.'

'Where are you reading that?'

'Look at their badge. I also recognise the number from an ad Hannah had on her computer.'

'Cool. Well, I'll give the hospital a call. Just wait right here.'

'Sure.'

I think about a million things I can do that will make them pay for the hurt that they put me through. But I did say to Jason that though they deserve this fate, I would save their lives, so I guess they can live. If they come back after me though, I shall not hesitate.

'Done, an ambulance is coming. They should be here in about ten minutes.'

'All right, so what should we do?'

'To be honest with you, I think we should either calm down this fire or get these two into a safer place.'

I stand up and look towards the fire, staring into the flames, my eyes following its movements.

'The dancing flames move like a wild spirit.'

'That's nice, Onyx.'

Jason stands up and walks up and stands beside me. I notice he stares at me for a little bit then holds my hand.

'Why did you come looking for me? After all, I'm the new girl who has strange abilities.'

'Well, even though you never wanted to be near me, I was always watching you. Don't get me wrong. I knew you were different, but I didn't care. You were you and had to fit into a society that sorts people into groups. Even though a group was chosen for me, I never accepted the label. I just accepted you.'

I felt tears bubbling up into my eyes then following the ride down my face and dripping off my chin.

'Onyx?'

'Thank you, Jason. I always said to myself that if I don't find someone that truly believes in me by the time

I'm eighteen, then I won't hesitate to hurt everyone and anyone who treated me wrongly.'

Jason says my name in what sounded to be a 'I feel so happy I met you' tone. Then he wraps his arms around me and gives me a huge comforting hug.

The next thing we hear is the siren of the ambulance, coming a lot earlier than expected. They lift the scientists into the ambulance then drive away after asking Jason and me what happened. We didn't lie, but we didn't say the whole truth either. All we said was that we were in the area when we saw the explosion and that we found these two people and helped them to the best of our abilities.

'Hey, Onyx.'

'Yeah, what is it, Jason?'

'When is your birthday?'

'Must you know?'

'Yes, I must know. When is it?'

'It's Thursday, 17 September.'

'The 17th? Wait a second, that's tomorrow!'

'Yeah, so?'

'Oh, nothing.'

'When is yours?'

'It's on 3 November.'

'All right. Well, did you want to head back to the school?'

'I don't know. The principal sounded scared that I ran down the corridor after you. I'll tell you what. You have two choices—one, you come with me and we spend the whole rest of the day out and about so I can show you the town or we go back to the school and explain what happened.'

'Yeah, I think I will take the first idea.'

'All right, let's go.'

'How long is it to walk back into the city from here? I have no idea where I am.'

'Oh, we are about an hour's walk back to the school.'

'So that means the city is thirteen minutes away from that.'

'Around that.'

The day is amazing. I have never had so much fun with anyone in such a long time. It's fantastic to go out and have no one care about who we are. It has been a long time since I've trusted someone enough to let them in. I didn't think I would ever do it again. The man that raised me destroyed a lot of the trust I had for people. My naivety disappeared after he told me the truth about who he was.

We go to many different shops, like the sunglasses-and-hat shop, where we look like idiots with hats, from posh and tall to feathery and classy. The glasses are all in different colours and sizes. We go to a humongous clothes shop, where we dress in all types of clothes from bright, frilly, and humiliating to dark, depressing, and weird. Jason holds my hand most of the time, and as we sit down and have fried rice from a nearby Chinese store, he asks me if I would be his girlfriend. I have never had this much compassion for someone for a long time, and I say yes to him. He even walks me home—well, you know, to the orphanage.

'Onyx, I have had the most fun today with you. I hope I can do this with you again soon.'

'I'm sure you will be able to, but next time, I might show you what I do in my spare time. I can even show you places in the school where students won't dare to go.'

'Sure, I would like that.'

He leans in and gives me a kiss on my cheek. I guess this is a scene that you would see on those romantic movies. All I know is that I have never felt happier, and I'm with someone who seems to genuinely care.

'Aunty Jo, I'm home. Aunt Jo! Where are you?'

'I'm up here, sweetie. What's the matter?'

'Oh, you started to get me worried there. What are you doing up here, Aunty Jo?'

'Oh, well, you see, I have this habit of coming to high places to think.'

'Why's that?'

'I love how the wind makes my shawl and long silver braid dance. It is a magical feeling, almost as if I can jump and soar with the wind. Oh, tut, tut, what am I saying? I better get down and start making the children afternoon tea for when they come home from school. Onyx, why are you home from school early today?'

'Oh, I thought you would want help, so I used my free time to come here. I have another idea, Aunt Jo. Why don't you stay up here for while? I'll take care of the afternoon tea and get the activities set up.'

'Thank you, Onyx. I would like that a lot.'

'That's all right. See you later, Aunt Jo.'

The children have so much fun with the different board games and hopscotch games; some even go and play basketball in the backyard. My happy phase ends as night falls. I'm sitting quietly on the roof, letting my long jacket and hair flow with the wind. My eyes are gazing at the full moon, and the clouds are drifting over one another.

The wait for the sun to rise in seven hours is killing me, for I have the fear of the SOMMIT. What move are they planning next? Have they finished with their search or not? Then I have the fear of tomorrow and now the stress of a boyfriend. Maybe it was not a good idea to say yes to Jason. Was I just flowing with the moment? It does raise an issue of how well I can protect someone that I have become a friend to. Maybe I should just enjoy this moon and wind before I stress out.

You know, sitting up here is very peaceful and relaxing. I guess stuff like this is the life of a stray who can always find a place that makes them feel at home. I lie down along the edge where I'm sitting, using my arms as a sort of pillow. I drift off to sleep, wondering what awaits me tomorrow.

'Onyx, wake up. You should get ready for school.'

'Oh, Aunt Jo, what's the time? Am I late?'

'No, dear, it's six o'clock. You slept up here all night and didn't hear your alarm.'

'Oh, thank you, Aunt Jo. I'll get ready.'

'That's a girl.'

I don't really wish to get ready, but I guess I should see the damage caused by the SOMMIT and me. I change into rolled-up three-quarter navy pants and a collared maroon shirt. I put on some black shoes and my knee-length black jacket. Then I prepare the breakfast for the children, just how they like it, and leave the house at 7.30 a.m. I took to the roofs this morning, so I can have the morning winds rush through my hair as I jump from rooftop to rooftop, running and racing with the wind. It feels like I can fly as I jump, but then I slow down so I can view the work at the school. There are at least five construction workers out front, and two have just walked in with the principal. I wonder how much trouble I'm going to get into.

'Principal Glosten!'

She turns around, shocked and surprised, as if she has seen a ghost. She has wide eyes, and her mouth is slightly agape.

'Hi, I wanted to come and say that I am sorry about yesterday. I want to explain exactly what happened. Is that okay?'

'Uh, yes, yes . . . excuse us.'

We walk into the nearest classroom at quite a fast pace for a short stumpy woman. I pretty much give her my life story from what I can remember to bring Principal Glosten up to date.

'Onyx, I . . . I would like you to stay with us here at Franklin High. You have said so much that can only be expected from the life of assassins or something you see in movies. I have not met anyone before that has endured the traumas you have.'

'You want me to stay?'

'Yes, why does that surprise you?'

'I just thought that I was going to be expelled.'

'No, but I will make sure that we support your abilities here.'

'Tha-thank you. I . . . I don't know what to say.'

'Well, I should go and tell those construction workers that the scientists did all the damage and how they did it. We will sit down and have a proper chat later, okay?'

'All right, see you later, Principal Glosten.'

'Onyx, take care, and I'll see you in class.'

CHAPTER 5

Damage Control

She leaves the classroom, leaving me absolutely speechless. I have a million things running through my head at once. What will the students think now that they know what I am? Is it still a good idea not to say anything to Jason? Now the school is getting fixed from the damage of the SOMMIT, and I still have that number that was written on the Internet ad. Is the number connected with the main place where all the creatures are kept? Who knows, the next few days may be hard to go through. For now, I think I shall keep a low profile.

The idea for surviving the rest of the week is to keep high on the rooftops for my lunch breaks. The moment the last bell of the day chimes, I'll go straight home to help Aunt Jo out. During classes, I should stay focussed on completing my work without saying anything. Already I can imagine how everyone would be. The teachers will not know how to look at me. The students will most likely avoid me. For now, I want to exile myself to spare being more exiled and feared than I ever have been.

The rest of the week cannot come quickly enough. For the weekend, all I want to do is stay in the orphanage. I want to hide from everyone, just get through the rest of this year so I can leave school. I have the rest of the year to figure out what I am going to do with the rest of my life. This won't be easy at all.

As I reach school this fine Thursday morning, I decide to scatter to the rooftops at the south wall. Students are lingering around the school, waiting for the bell to go in half an hour since it is only 8 a.m. I see Hannah and Marsha getting a drink from the fountains and laughing away as if nothing had happened.

I think of maybe using my speed to drop her water bottle on her head so that her clothes will be wet for the entire day. She would know it was me though since I am the only one wearing a jacket this long; it would look like a cape at my speed. What I can do is keep an eye out for any SOMMIT activity while I'm up here. Also, I should keep an eye on Hannah, Marsha, as well as Jason since he will probably be looking for me. I've told Aunt Jo that if anyone comes looking for me, she can tell them that I've left yesterday and I'm heading back to Transylvania in Louisiana.

That makes me wonder, what if Jason travels to Transylvania? He can get into a lot of trouble asking about me there. Ever since they found out who and what I am, they have been keeping an eye out for the SOMMIT just in case I'd ever come back.

Oh yeah, this is nice and relaxing, almost like last night, except I have no moon, just the shadows peering over on the south tower. I'm high enough that no one can see me and I can see everyone. Hannah and Marsha have gone and joined the cheerleaders and the jocks who are sitting on benches underneath a few trees. I see Jason walk up to them with his Franklin High jacket, which represents that he is a football jock. He walks up to Brian, Hannah, and Marsha, who quickly join him.

Jason throws the jacket on to the grass in front of them, stands on it, and then walks away. Hannah is trying to calm down Brian, who wants to have a go at Jason; he manages to scream out for the entire school to hear.

'Hey, Jason! I heard that your feral girl was captured by those scientists then taken away to be chopped up.'

'Shows what you know! She escaped yesterday!'

'Oh, really? Look again, because she isn't here. And if you know that she escaped, then where is she?'

'She is . . . uh . . .'

'Oh, the little ex-jock doesn't know where his feral cat is. Have you looked in a dumpster?'

That's it. I am going to show an appearance for everyone to remember.

I jump down and utilise my speed, dashing toward Jason and Brian, who are moving closer to go at it. Just a little bit more, and I will be able to stand between them and knock Brian on his ass. I aim to push him back by using my momentum to hit his chest slightly. That's all it needs to be since I don't really want to hurt the guy.

Well, I don't want to get into trouble since the school's damage is my fault.

'That's enough!' I snap when jumping between them.

'Huh?' gasps Jason.

'Ahh! Arggh,' complains Brian.

'Brian!' screams Hannah.

I hold my hand out to Jason so he won't run into me. They're moving pretty quickly towards each other, but I'm quicker.

'That does it! Stop this, both of you! Brian, I am not some animal! I have the eyes of a cat as well as its abilities and senses, not to mention the ferocity of a cat, but I am at this moment very tame. So if you wish to see me furious, then keep trying to annoy me or my boyfriend!'

Gasps go round the crowd, and I realise what I've said. It's like the word *vomit*. It's something you cannot recall the moment it's instinctually said. I try to take it back, but Marsha takes the spotlight.

'Your boyfriend? Who could that possibly be, the stray tabby cat that roams around here from time to time?'

Laughter starts from the viewers, who're wondering if there's going to be a fight. I glare at Marsha, and I'm about ready to pounce.

'No, you morons. *I'm* Onyx's boyfriend.'

'Jason!' gasps Marsha with her eyes wide. 'No, no, no, no, no . . . this can't be! Since when? Why?'

'Marsha, you're going to hurt your brain. Did you not get the idea that I do not like you?'

She screams then walks off, trying to help Hannah with her winded boyfriend. I walk off too in the opposite direction, leaving a very confused Jason. I think he's thinking about how close he was to having a fight.

I would have let them be if it was just over him leaving the team but those words were at me, piercing my eardrums, turning my eyes bright yellow with rage. I walk around the corner where I can jump back up to the south tower. Any second later, and I would have had given my position away to Jason, who wants to catch up to me. It's not like I'm avoiding him, but I just do not wish to talk to him at the moment. None of them are in geography today, so maybe I can think it over then.

For now, I think I will have a nice, relaxing catnap on the roof. Huh? Oh, man, it feels like I have only just closed my eyes, and now the bell has rung. Great, some grey clouds are to the west. I wonder if we are going to get some rain. Who knows? Oh well, best be off to form class. Just like the first day when I entered the room of C2, the whispers and murmurs come to a sudden stop, and eyes glare straight at me.

The teacher, Miss Gardner, stops in her place and has to shake herself out of the trance. She then tells the rest of the class the quick daily notices. I walk to sit down where I usually sit in the third row on the far left side. As I walk past Jason, he passes me a rectangular blue box. I sit down at my seat and open the box that has a 'Happy Birthday' card in it. The card reads,

To Onyx,

Happy birthday!

I shall always be by your side no matter what happens. Hope you have a great birthday, and I hope you like the present.

Jason

Behind the card is a custom-made collar made out of leather, just like the one I am currently wearing. This one has a silver cat head for decoration on it, with green cat-shaped eyes that look very tame but ferocious. I swap my black leather collar with this exquisite navy-blue leather one that Jason gave me. The bell rings just as I put my old collar around my boot.

'Do you like the present, birthday girl?'

'Yes, thank you, Jason.'

'It suits you.'

'Well, I best be off to class. I'm looking forward to geography. Thanks again for the gift. I really like it.'

Everything is awkward now ever since yesterday when I said yes. Maybe it is best for everyone if I leave again.

'Sit down, class, and welcome to year 12 geography. I will be your teacher, Mr O'Neil. This term, we are going to study the rainforests and Antarctica. Let's open up our books and get started. Do chapters 7.1 through to 7.8 of your textbooks.'

After seventy long minutes, the class is over, and I head for my second class, maths, where I waste my entire class on doing one page out of the three pages given to us. It is lunchtime, and I am safely on the north tower, just where I was when I came on my first day. I decide to bring Jason up with me this time; it's not hard since all I have to do is pick him up and jump just like I usually do.

'Onyx, why has it been so awkward . . . talking to you?'

'I don't know. I think because we have skipped a step and was just flowing with the moment yesterday.'

'Do you think we should stay as we were, as friends?'

'It may be easier since, well, with the SOMMIT still out and about, I may not be able to stay in one place for too long.'

'That's understandable. Do you want to go speak to the scientists that we blew up yesterday?'

'Yeah, we can go after school one day. I'm still unsteady and wish to see them suffer.'

'Uh . . . cool. Now if I ever want to get up here without feeling like a loser because a girl has to pick me up, can I?'

'Uh . . . you might need help till we find a way.'

'That is fair enough, but for real, what do you think we should do now that the entire school thinks we are going out?'

'Hmmm, well, I suppose we can keep it like it is, because it is sometimes nice to talk to someone.'

'Yeah, sweet.'

'But I just want to let you know that I don't do the physical stuff and I need my space. I guess it is true.'

'What is?'

'I am exactly like a stray cat.'

'Eh?'

Hmmm, I look up to the clouds above with a smile, thinking of how nice it is to relax even though hell is waiting just below us.

'Hey, Jason . . .'

'What is it, Onyx?'

'How well are you in climbing up walls if you hold a rope?'

'Oh, well, if it's like rock climbing, then I shall have no problems. Why do you ask?'

'I know how to get you up here when I'm not around to help you. Also if I place it just right, then no one else should be able to get it.'

'Get what?'

'Well, I was thinking of grabbing some climbing rope and securing it to a pre-planned position up here. Then I'll make sure it's long enough for you to grab and climb to a nearby window or something. That way, all it takes is you climbing up the rope.'

'That is actually a really good idea. I have an idea on which window you can use. If you ask Principal Glosten, she may give us a spare key for the window just off the south wall. I am pretty sure it's an old classroom that doesn't get used. I noticed that the south wall is covered in shade for most of the day and the wind is mild from how the building is situated. The window I'm on about is that one there. It is about halfway between the tower's roof to this roof that we're standing on now. I have some old rock climbing gloves, so I would have grip. As you go up, you can see for decoration some bits of metal that look like they are secured by the cement. Old iron steps,

I think. All we will have to do is secure the rope up there, and we are in business. I noticed that, from the south wall, you can travel easy enough to the western side of the school, where the roof shades you for the afternoon, and in the morning, we can maybe make it to the east side of the school since it is shady only in the mornings. The north tower, I won't be able to get to, so if you want, that can be your getaway area. My dad has some old rock-climbing rope from when we used to scale cliffs. I'm sure he won't mind.'

'Uh! That is actually quite smart, Jason. And can you ask Principal Glosten about the key? I'm still unsure how she truly thinks after everything. Once everything is sorted, I'll hook it all up.'

'Great. Well, let's go. The bell will go off in about five minutes.'

'All right, come on. Are you ready?'

'Good thing I'm not scared of heights.'

Although I'm unsure about what to do next, it feels rather nice just being a student and knowing that at least two people want me to stay in the school. I'm in the principal's office for the rest of the day because she wants to have a heart-to-heart chat about the SOMMIT. Amazingly, that conversation doesn't last long. We actually spend most of the time talking about what to do and say to the school. Since the classrooms on the south side of the school have been trashed, we come up with an idea for my own personal classroom, where no one can see inside and no one can hear the words that come from inside the room.

I have to keep it clean as cleaners' won't be able to access it. I'm also allowed to invite whomever I want. Once permissions are granted, Principal Glosten agrees to our idea of gaining access to the roof. I think she appreciates the safety aspects so that no one will be stranded up there. Jason and I do some remodelling to the wall so we can utilise it. The best part is that there are only three keys to the room. There is a key for Jason, Principal Glosten, and I. Inside the classroom, we have a tiny fridge, some desks, and chairs for other students like me, if there actually will be other students like me.

A blackboard and whiteboard are located on the front wall. Due to the amount and type of construction, we come up with an agreement with the construction workers to have full freedom of the school while the students take the time off. Five days are agreed to for majority of the fixtures to be sorted. Students are told to leave and come back on Wednesday, 22 September. The time off is good, and it allows my mind to focus on the orphanage and set up the climbing rope for Jason. He helps a fair bit with his knowledge on how to have it and secure it.

Now it's time to focus on school. Knowing that I have a getaway from the other students make me feel like I can get through the year easier. Principal Glosten gives us the key after she inspects the set-up of the classroom and the climbing rope. The busy five days come to a screeching halt as I wake to the morning of the 22nd.

School is back, and the cheerleaders and jocks seem to spend a lot more time together than usual, suspiciously glaring at me any chance they get. After a week back at school, Jason and I find out why.

The eight o'clock bell rings, and we climb up our rope system into our classroom. When we go out to the hallway, there are hundreds of pictures hanging up—on the door, walls, floor, everywhere you look. They are of animals and people from magazines that have been cut out and placed together to create human-and-animal abominations, as the SOMMIT calls us.

There are so many pictures, and my blood is boiling. I do not know what I should do. Jason starts to rip down the pictures, but there are so many that Jason cannot hide the sight of them. The photos we saw at the SOMMIT warehouse came jumping back into my mind. Something is occurring and my nails suddenly grow longer and my canine teeth start to grow. Jason must have seen what was happening. He'd seen this before.

Laughter from the cheerleaders and jocks grows louder in my ears, echoing constantly. Sounds around me are starting to sound muffled. It's so strange; my heart begins pounding, and I'm scared about what's happening to me. I don't understand. The SOMMIT creeps at every corner of my mind, along with all the harm they have caused to others.

I lower my head and close my eyes, using my hands to cover my ears just to try to get the sounds and images out of my head. Suddenly, I hear a voice in the darkness of my mind. No, wait, not my mind. I know this voice. It's Jason. I should listen . . . shouldn't I?

'Onyx . . .' Muffled.

'Onyx, Onyx! Snap out of it!'

His arms are around my arm, and I feel sick. He turns me around and drags me into our classroom. He pushes me inside and turns around to lock the door. I fall straight to the floor and remember nothing else of the real world.

CHAPTER 6

Memory Lane

'What is going on? Where am I? Wait, is that a little girl? Hey, you, what is going on? Where are we?'

The little girl looks at me; she looks about six years old, wearing a long black jacket that drags a good couple of inches on the ground. She has it wrapped around her as if it comforts her. Although the jacket is long, her sleeves are slightly rolled up to her wrists, and there are red gloves on her.

No, wait. My eyes widen as I notice that the red gloves are not gloves at all. The red runs down her fingertips and drips to the ground. I look closer at her innocent face. Her long jet-black hair has been neatly brushed, and her eyes look sad—not the sad as if she wishes to cry, but sad as if she wants her life to be different. The dark background changes its appearance to an old-designed brick house. It looks like the girl and I were in a backyard filled with colourful flowers and a cobblestone path.

'What's going on?'

The girl does not reply to me. She just looks at me then runs down the cobblestone path.

'Hey, wait!'

Where is this girl going? I ask myself as I follow her. This path seems endless, and the little girl just keeps on running. I decided to walk, as I don't think, I'm moving forward. Frankly, I have no clue why I'm following her. She disappears now around a corner of a grey brick wall.

When I finally reach the wall, I walk around and see a magnificent fountain, the kind that you will only see in fairy tales. The young girl is sitting on the edge, placing her fingertips in the water, watching how the blood swirls with each turn and ripple. Slowly I walk up to talk to her; she stands up and skips on the edge, skipping a few steps then turning around and skipping back.

'Hey, you, uh . . . little girl.'

She stops and stares then gives me a cute, innocent smile. 'Glistens the water a stain of red. Follow your mind from a life you dread.'

'What . . . what do you mean, little girl?'

'Glistens the water a stain of red; Follow your mind from a life you dread.'

What on earth! She jumps into the fountain. Does she intend to kill herself? I run up to the fountain and look over at the unsteady water, desperately looking for the girl; no noise and no bubbles appear as the water starts to calm, showing my frightened expression. Wait, I can hear something in the water! I peer ever closer at the calm water, listening for the little girl's voice. I look around, but there is no sign of anyone. The voice gets louder, and I realise that the girl is singing.

One phrase is sung repeatedly. 'Glistens the water a stain of red. Follow your mind from a life you dread.'

What does it mean in a situation like this? Wait, what is that? A black shape is in the water. Is that the girl? I launch my hand into the water, attempting to grab her out. No! I must put my hand in deeper. The water is reaching my shoulder when I feel her ice-cold hand touch mine. At first, I feel relieved that I have a hold of this girl and have the strength to pull her up. My expression of happiness changes to fear as I feel myself getting pulled in by the little girl. This is so strange. Any moment, I am going to be in the water. Why is she going to drown me?

Given the amount of time she has been underwater; I am surprised that she is still conscious. She pulls and pulls until I give in and feel a cool sensation pour over me. My eyes close, and my body drifts in the water. The little girl's hand holds me tight, and she takes me deeper and deeper. I open my eyes after I feel something rub against my cheek.

Jason? No, it's that little girl.

It feels like we have been underwater for ages, but when I look back up to where we came from, I see something very familiar.

'Glistens the water a stain of red. Follow your mind from a life you dread.'

'Huh, that phrase, what does it mean?'

'Look up to the sky above. Find what keeps your heart from love.'

'Look up, you say?'

What will I possibly see up in the sky above me? And the last sentence: 'Find what keeps my heart from love.' Strange girl, but I have curiosity running through my veins as I tilt my head up to gaze where the sun glistens down upon the little girl and I.

Wait, what is this? I ask myself as my eyes widen and my jaw drops. That's me from the other night, sitting on the orphanage rooftop. But what is happening to me? I . . . I am getting younger, almost as if I'm watching myself from now to when I was born—but surely not. No way, the image of me stops at a certain point, and I realise that this little girl looks exactly like I did when I was her age. Wait a second . . .

'Time is but an invention made by man. Time and age join in the centre hand in hand.'

'Uh, so I'm right. You're me.'

'Spirit to spirit, heart to heart, time will never keep them apart.'

'Hey, can you speak properly little . . . uh . . . little me? Hang on, I know these rhymes.'

One more is needed to be said. So far we have 'Glistens the water a stain of red. Follow your mind from a life you dread. Look up to the sky above. Find what keeps your heart from love. Time is but an invention made by man. Time and age join in the centre hand in hand. Spirit to spirit, heart to heart, time will never keep them apart.'

Oh, what's the last one? Let's see—memory, heart, time . . . and blood! That's it! 'The smell of blood will never be forgotten. The blood does not remain, but it lies rotten.'

What's this, this feeling in my stomach?

'What . . . what did you do to me, you little girl?'

'I simply am here to remind you of something that has been forgotten in your *spirit*, *mind*, and *heart* over *time*. You have lost the true meaning in your *blood*.'

'What have I forgotten?'

'Your life.'

Her words have no emotion in them, exactly like her lifeless but innocent eyes. She disappears as if she has transformed into many bubbles, floating gracefully to the surface. I try to move, but my body stiffens. I'm not allowed to move from where I am.

Another vision appears in front of me, but this time, it shows me as the little girl getting younger to an infant being cared for by my two parents. It starts with a muscular figure with short brown hair; a short moustache grows from under his nose, which he rubs into the nose of the tiny baby girl. The baby has big bright-yellow and green eyes; she is wrapped in a white blanket, smiling and laughing happily.

A lovely woman appears with long black hair tied up into a braid. She has irregularly long nails and two cats' ears on her head. I look quickly again as this woman covers her ears with two pieces of bold-red ribbon. This woman grabs hold of the baby and rocks her calmly to sleep, then places her gently into a pram. The vision disappears for a moment, giving me time to think. I understand that the baby is me. This leaves me to assume that the two people are my parents. I don't really remember what my parents look like, so it's nice to see their faces once again.

This time, the scene is me on my first day of kindergarten. I'm wearing a knee-length black pleated skirt and an emerald-green V-neck shirt. I'm holding my mother's hand, and she drops me off at the centre and then leaves, heading back the way she came. My father's work is only a few blocks away, so after a day of sleeping, drinking milk, and colouring in, I walk over to the factory, where dad waits for me at the gate. On this particular day though, we have finished early because our caretaker has to leave due to her son breaking his arm at high school football.

I decide to go into the factory owned by my father. The factory is Michael's Magic Milk Makers. Lucky he married a cat lady, because I don't think anyone likes milk more than my family does. I sneak past Gerald, the main guard at the factory, and climb through a small window on the second floor.

My dad is yelling at someone in the shadows. He's saying very nasty things to this person. 'No, you stupid person! I shall not go against my orders again. I have told you more than enough times to never come to this factory. You must always stay home and keep yourself hidden. Now that you have come, everyone knows about you, and thanks to the devices in here, we have to terminate this issue immediately!'

I look ever closer at everything and see that inside this factory, there is no milk or machines to make milk. My dad has lied to mum and me. I spot the badge my dad wears; it states, 'Michael Limestone, founder of Michael's Magic Milk Makers. Call 55436251.' Although my dad is holding a white coat, the badge on the coat states, 'Michael Limestone, member of SOMMIT. Call 55682142.'

Gunshots are fired towards the person in the shadows. All that my eyes see are flickers of light from the gunfire and a woman with fine black hair and a pretty ribbon for decoration. She's wearing a lovely black dress with knee-high black stockings.

When I realised who this familiar person is, the gunshot echoes vanished from my ears, and my heart begins to race. Something is occurring, my nails suddenly grow longer and my canine teeth start to lengthen, not to mention my ears are disappearing and feline ears are growing on the top of my head. I turn around to go out the window, terrified. I see my reflection. I look fierce and more like a cat than a human.

I feel my heart ache, and I know that the blood boiling inside my body means that I want revenge on my father. I black out after this, but all the pictures show bodies slaughtered and lying mangled on the ground.

I'm covered in blood, and my father is in front of me, holding his bleeding right arm. Feeling weak, my more-human form returns. I start to feel weak in the knees, and I collapse to the ground, barely able to open my eyes. I feel someone grab me. Looking up, I see it's Michael, my own father. He's looking at me with eyes saying, 'You disgusting filthy animal.' A man's voice flows through my body, sending shivers up my spine.

'Finish the animal. Your wife at least has been taken care of, so let's kill off the family.'

'Not yet, Henry. First, I must take out a beating on this child for killing our comrades.'

'Do as you wish. Just make sure that she is reminded how we hate her kind.'

'Yes, the purpose of the SOMMIT is to study and exterminate these pests. I had almost forgotten.'

'Why don't you knock some sense into her, then take her home, and remind her why she is a pitiful, disgusting creature?'

'You hear that, daughter, eh? You are not of this world and must be treated harshly. It's not like you're human, so we can do whatever is considered inhuman to you.'

My father has a nasty smile on his face. I feel as if I'm looking at the most wicked person on the planet. He hits me repeatedly with as much force as possible into each blow. I do not know how much longer my body is going to last before something breaks. His words keeps saying to forget my mother, forget what she looks like, forget she was even born. I cannot bear any more, but my shrieks of pain do not make them feel sorrow. They do nothing more than laugh. Closing my eyes, I try to picture my mum so I will never forget her.

I wake up on my small bed; my clothes and body are covered in blood. My arms and legs are chained to the bed so I cannot move. I hear in the distance my father talking to Henry about what they're going to do. Henry gives Dad three days to kill me, and then he is to return to the SOMMIT.

The door slams shut, and Dad comes barging through my door.

'So you are awake, Onyx. Onyx, your mother died at birth, understand? You killed a lot of my comrades, and I will never forgive you for that. Those chains are to stop you from moving or turning into that animal that lurks inside you. If you ever bare those fangs at me again, I will not hesitate again on killing you. I am the top member of the organisation known as SOMMIT—Science of Military, Magical, Interesting Things. We started ninety-seven years ago when we first spotted a fairy dancing in the Canadian mountains. My best skill is inhuman treatment, and you shall be no exception to the rest that we have studied and disposed of. Now, Onyx, my job is simple, but today, you reminded me too much of your mother . . . I may let you live longer than three days, but even though you are like your mother in features, I will treat you how I have felt these last few years, you disgusting creature.'

He walks out, leaving me to fall gently back into a deep sleep. My mind ventures through, replaying what had occurred at the factory. As the days go by, all my father does is hit me and curse at my existence. I feel so alone now that I'm the only one like me, my mother, is dead, but I'm not allowed to think about my mother. I just need to know that she died shortly after my birth. I blame my father as a scientist from the SOMMIT.

That one word, *SOMMIT,* sends shivers all over my body; it's scary that they mistreat people like me. Seven days have gone by, and my body is covered in bruises.

It hurts to breathe or move. I probably have broken or fractured bones. I'm only allowed to change my clothes once to knee-length maroon shorts and a blue T-shirt. I have barely eaten or had anything to drink. I am only allowed to move to go to the bathroom.

Dad has a visit from Henry on what I think is the eighth day; I'm locked in the bathroom. He charges in, searching the place with many other people. Father is shouting at Henry for his incompetence and lack of patience. I lean next to the door, trying to listen how far away they are from me.

'Michael, you are such a fool, keeping that whelp alive. The boss will not be happy about this and will kill you for this. Did you or did you not keep that filthy animal alive?'

'I . . . uh . . .'

'Men, keep searching! Michael is no longer a SOMMIT member and must be terminated.'

'Yes, sir.'

'Henry, you traitor, you took the position as secretary, didn't you?'

'Well, Michael, if you must know, yes. Yes, I did.'

'Then I guess there is one last mission for me if I'm not part of this organisation. With this gun, I shall kill you!'

CHAPTER 7

Bloodline

I hear many shots fired and things falling and breaking. I hear footsteps all clustering to one area of the house. I slip on the tiles and hit the door, making a bang echo throughout the house. I shake in fear as I wait for the men to come and find me; my movements are slight as I slowly make my way to a standing position. Feet are pounding all along the wooden floors, making it almost impossible to figure out where they are. The doorknob rattles in front of me, and the men come to investigate.

'Sir, the door is locked, and we have confirmed that this is the bathroom.'

'Knock it down, and find out why it has been locked,' replies Henry.

I hide in the darkest corner I could find in the white-painted walls. I listen and wait as I shut my eyes and hear the wood starting to chip away. Any moment now, and they shall have this door open; they will find me and probably kill me.

'Got ya, girlie!'

'Ahh! No, let me go!'

'And why would we do that, you filthy brat?'

'Because I don't have to be treated so wrongly, do I?'

'You know what, you are very smart and mature for your age. But I know what will make you grow up faster.'

Henry is a man who looks to be at the age of early forties. He has no facial hair, but his thin dark-brown hair has segments of grey from old age, I guess. He has a devilish smile on him, and it makes me cower in fear just by looking into his eyes. His hazelnut-brown eyes are lifeless at first glance. As I look longer, I can almost feel the amount of kills he has done in his life. He almost has his eyes dancing just at the thought of killing, especially me because I'm not human.

I look over his shoulder to see my dad holding his stomach. Those shots that were fired hit a nearby vase, and Henry must have fired a shot because my father had been hit by a bullet in his stomach. I shriek and run down to him. It's not like my father will care, but I guess, he is still my father. I rush past the couch and kneel down beside him.

'Get away, you filthy vermin! I don't need your pity.'

'You know what, I have had it with you, Father, and your stupid SOMMIT. There is no way I will die here today, and there is no way that I am ever going to be mistreated by you all again.'

As I keep rambling on, I don't notice Henry and his men coming behind me. They grab me, pinning me to the floor.

'What a lovely speech for an animal, but listen, kid, you are in no place to say this. Anyway, I now have in my possession a traitor and an abomination. Whatever shall I do? I know! Code 7692.'

'Yes, sir.'

The men grab me and pin me down on the couch, facing my father. What are they planning to do? What is code 7692?

Henry crouches down to my father and whispers in his ear; unfortunately, all I can hear is my heart racing. For all those under fifteen, I highly suggest you skip this next scene. This is not a vital point in my life, but it is part of the reason I am like myself today.

My eyes are forced upon my father, and I watch him being decapitated by a strange-looking thirty-centimetre sword; my father is killed by one of his fellow comrades, Henry. My screams do not disturb anyone from the SOMMIT, nor does it get anyone's attention outside the walls of my house that was covered in blood. My head is held tightly as I'm forced to look at my father's remains; in the end, all I can do is close my eyes and scream.

'For pity's sake, just shut up!'

Henry is so angry at my high level of noise that he begins kicking me repeatedly, making me tremble and cough out a lot of blood. I'm almost certain that this is going to be the end for me. I collapse to the floor, barely able to breathe. Is there going to be more suffering before they just dispose of me like some piece of garbage? I'm sure that just a few more hits and I would be out of existence—not that anyone in the world would care that

I'm gone. It's not as if I've started a life yet. I mean, I have not even reached primary school.

'Wait!' says someone that just barged through the door. I'm too tired to care, but at least I'm still alive even if it's just for a few minutes longer.

'The chancellor has requested we keep this whelp alive and go by his orders of code 6675. Apparently, this is a special one, for this girl has the bloodline from the great cat demons, the one that has the family tree that dates back to ancient Egypt.'

'Wait, are you telling me that this child is a descendant of Egyptian rulers?'

'Yes, that is why you must follow his orders.'

'Yes, sir, right away. May I ask where the keeper is.'

'At the location.'

'Okay, men, you heard him. Let's get this girl to the location.'

Those are the last words of Henry and the last time I see him due to the fact that someone behind me hits my head with a baton. When I come to, a man is putting a facecloth on my head. My eyes widen, and I try to sit up, but my body becomes dizzy and disorientated.

'Hey, hey, don't you worry now. Just calm yourself down, and I'll explain so you might get a better understanding of what happened to you.'

What am I supposed to do? My body is not going to let me move no matter how hard I try.

'Okay, well, let's start with names. My name is Charlie. I run a business at the local shooting range. I am known as a gun expert by many. Now your turn.'

'I . . . I, my name's Onyx . . . Onyx Limestone. I go to the Hamilton Street kindergarten.'

'All right, Onyx, well, do you want me to tell you how you came to be in my possession?'

I nod him my reply since I have no energy to speak any more than what I already have.

'Okay, well, I was walking back from an apartment when I saw a bunch of guys in white coats carrying you into an alleyway. As far as I could see, you were covered in bruises, and that was when I knew you did not belong to them. I had a .25 handgun that I keep on me at all times, so I threatened them with it and took you into my possession. I have been caring for you for three days now.'

My eyes widen as I see the innocence in his face, which makes me feel very safe. Slowly I'm off in a daze in the black sea of dreams.

The scene ends, and we enter to when I was fourteen years old. I'm calmly sitting on the roof of a one-story brick house that holds three bedrooms and has five acres, allowing us to practice shooting. I'm staring off at the streets, where the peak-hour traffic of 4 p.m. was coming home. Charlie has been very kind to me. He has paid for all my school studies throughout primary school, and I am currently in high school. I feel like I have met someone who actually cares for me.

I have lived so long with him now that we have built up a great relationship. We can talk about anything, and Charlie knows me so well, he can tell everything about me, whether I am happy, or sad, or if I just wish to talk about something on my mind. Charlie is like a friend or the father that I truly wanted. He's even taught me how to fire a simple handgun, but I'm not much of a gun person, so I do not like to shoot.

A bell rings an hour later, and I have Charlie calling for me, saying that dinner is ready. I jump down to eat the delicious meal of chicken breast steaks and fried rice.

'Onyx, I think it's time I tell you something about the SOMMIT.'

'Eh?'

'Well, the SOMMIT are always around, and they have started a huge organisation. They will be after you, Onyx.'

'I know, but I don't know much about them or why they are after me. It was so long ago.'

'There are a few things that you might want to know. I am an undercover agent working for the SOMMIT. I have been assigned to care for you and study you in a natural environment. I am not supposed to kill you, but after this next sentence, you may want to kill me. I am the chancellor for the SOMMIT in this area. This means that I knew about your mother's true catlike form. So I set up the plot for her to go to the factory and get herself killed. What I wasn't planning on was seeing you as strong as you are, so then I planned the assault on your father and took you under my wing so I could keep a close eye on you.'

'Eh'

My mind goes blank, and my body stiffens. I've always thought Charlie is the one person who understands me. The one person I trust ends up being the very person who wants to study me. My vision goes blurry, and I stand up, trying to run with a disoriented feeling. I manage to get to the front veranda leading out to the backyard. My body is so confused, and my mind just needs time to unravel all the information it just received.

I pass out, landing on the wooden veranda. I don't really know what will happen, but as my eyes close, I see Charlie's feet walk up to me. My mind is at the verge of not transmitting anything. I hear a soft voice in the background. My head is pounding, and I have no idea of the day or time. I don't think my body will move even if I want it to.

'Onyx, wakey-wakey.'

'Who's there?'

'Just me, Onyx. There's no need to worry.'

My eyes focus, showing that Charlie is sitting in a chair about five metres from where I am. As I look around, I notice that I'm lying on the old couch situated on the veranda.

'Onyx, why did you pass out?'

'I . . . I don't know.'

'Are you all right?'

'I thi-think so.'

'Are you still disoriented?'

'Now I remember. You tried to kill me, right?'

'No, I told you the truth, and you ran off, then collapsed. Now, Onyx, you are like a daughter to me. So I am going to do something I don't usually do. You are allowed to leave, but we will be in pursuit very soon. So as soon as you are better, you will leave, and I will be in pursuit. Or you can stay and volunteer with the SOMMIT.'

Huh, what is he talking about? He is not going to kill me or study me? He thinks that I am like his daughter, so I'm allowed to leave? I guess I'll just go to that Transylvania that I like to read about at school. But that's an easy few days' drive from here. Will I be able to get away?

The darkness rushes, and I'm back under the water with barely any light. The sun looks so far away. I feel movement in my body, and as I look around, I realise that I have forgotten a lot in my life. With this information, I remember that I ran off to Transylvania, Louisiana, and spent two and a half years of my life there.

Sadly, though it is only a matter of time till the SOMMIT chases you down and tries to get you. When I moved to Salem, I thought that I wouldn't make good friends with anyone. I thought my life was going to be a huge chase around the world until I was too old or too tired. At least I can call this place home.

More movement comes into my body, and I'm back in control. As soon as I realise this, my breath gives in, and I need air. I drastically try to swim to the surface, but I'm too deep in the fountain to make it. The bottom is nowhere in sight, so I can't even use that to help me reach the surface. Maybe that girl is here to kill me. What do I do now? I don't really want to die. I want to live a life of my own without the SOMMIT. I feel my body being crushed by the pressure of the water, and I know that I only have a little bit of time until I lose consciousness.

After that happens, I'll drown. I close my eyes since it's too hard to keep them open. I let my mind do as my body and just drift with the flow of the water. My ears feel the unbearable pain from the pressure.

I hear a voice. I wondered who it is. Is it my mother or someone else I know? As I listen, the pressure subsides, and the voice gets louder and louder till I can hear the muffled voice turning into a plain voice right in front of me.

CHAPTER 8

Understanding

'Onyx! Hey Onyx, are you all right?'

I sit up quickly, breathing deeply to get the flow of oxygen back into my lungs. After a short moment, I look around and realise I'm back in Salem, back in our classroom.

'Jason, have you been watching over me the whole time?'

'Most of the time. I left to talk to Principle Glosten. I locked the door when I left, and also the cheerleaders and jocks are getting in trouble for the fiasco they did at first period.'

'What's the time now?'

'It's just gone past 11.30 a.m.'

'Eleven thirty! Gosh, that means—wait, I remember it was about 8 a.m. when we left to go to form. That means I have been out of it for three and a half hours.'

'Yes, and Principal Glosten will be in to check on us later. She was last here at 10 a.m.'

'Okay, I understand. I'm glad that we are all safe and not drowning.'

'Drowning?' asked Jason.

'Yeah, don't worry. It's a long story.'

'Hey, Onyx, are you all right?'

'Yeah, just tired. I think my brain has consumed too much information.'

'Well, okay, but you should tell your parent about the situation between the SOMMIT and the school.'

'Parent?'

'Yeah, Principal Glosten said that your parental guardian is Aunt Jo.'

'Oh, well, she should know the whole truth, I suppose.'

'Yeah.'

'Oh, and Jason, what did you do about all those photos?'

'Gyaa, I . . . I asked the cleaner to take them down.'

I know I'm scaring him, but after my memory has been raised to the surface, I can't help but glare as furiously as a lion hunting its prey. My stomach is turning, and my heart is racing.

'How could you? Why didn't you do something about all this?'

'Wha-what was I supposed to do? I'm only one person. Tha-that was a lot of photos!'

'Well, you have proved it. You may not be a jock, but you are definitely a *human*!'

'Onyx, what are you talking about?'

'Humans are all the same. They care about themselves first.'

'Hang on, what on earth are you on about? Yes, I am human! I am glad I am, so I don't have to put up with stupid categories. I am my own person. I think it's about time you realise that you are also a person!'

'Gosh, how many times did you just use the word *I*? Why don't you try to be the outcast to the point you are beaten up and ridiculed? If you want to feel like a human, then don't talk to me. I witnessed my parents get murdered at four years of age. My mother was slaughtered by the SOMMIT—by none other than my father! He's a member of the SOMMIT, and he beat me when I didn't know that it was wrong, because he was my father!'

It was all just pouring out of me. I was so emotional that the rational side of me went on a sort of auto pilot. Jason didn't need to hear this, but I couldn't stop talking.

'Onyx, I had no idea, really . . .'

'I know you didn't. I only just remembered. You may not be a jock and just a human being. I have seen that, but I can't be protected by you since they wish to punish me for something I was born with. You saw the pictures. My kind has been slaughtered and treated inhumanly by people who think differently, and I officially can't take it anymore. But don't you dare underestimate me or take pity on me!'

'Onyx, I . . . I . . .'

'Shut up!' I run out of the room, seeing nothing but blackness, tears running down my face. All I feel is the wind and the movement of my body. Next thing I notice I'm waking up on the north tower, feeling disorientated and a massive headache. I look around and attempt to remember what's going on. I'm so confused, and I feel so lost.

'Onyx, if you are anywhere on the school premises, then I would like you to please go to room C7.'

I know that voice. It's Aunt Jo. How my heart sinks and my eyes soften at the sound of her calm voice. She's at—hang on, C7 is our classroom. I wobble my way across to the south wall and climb down into the window of the C7 classroom.

'Aunt Jo? Aunt Jo? Huh!'

'Onyx, your principal has explained the situation to me. I . . . I don't know what to say, really. I was worried when I heard . . . yet I understand.'

I can't help it; it's as if my heart is aching. Tears run down my cheeks and drip to the floor. I run towards Aunt Jo and hug her as tight as I could—without hurting her, of course.

'Aunt Jo, I am so sorry.'

'For what, Onyx?'

'I don't know. I just don't want to hurt you.'

'Shh there, it's all right.'

I fall to my knees, tired from exhaustion, and Aunt Jo holds me tight in her arms till I'd fallen asleep. When I wake, there's a piece of paper beside me signed by Aunt Jo. It says:

> I had to leave since it was nearing two o'clock. I wish to speak to you when you get home this afternoon. Take care.
>
> Aunt Jo

Well, at least my headache has disappeared, but I won't forget this day. Well, I need a drink. I wonder if the tuck shop is still open. I wander outside the classroom and down the empty halls out into the J block eating area, where the tuck shop is situated.

'Hi, deareh', what can I git ya this arvo?'

This is Doris, the lunch lady. She has that type of accent that makes her sound funny, but I guess that's just the Kiwi in her.

'Hi, Doris, um, do you have any bottles of milk left?'

'Ah, right ya are there, Onyx. Just found the last o' the cartons. Hope ya goteh' one dolla sixteh.'

'Yes, Doris.' I chuckle. 'One sixty right here.'

'Sweetahs', ain't ya a nice lass. Well, 'ere ya go. Take care now, ya 'ear?'

'See ya later. Thank you, Doris.'

As I wander back towards C7, I think about all the conversations Aunt Jo could speak to me about, especially after everything that has happened.

'Hey, look! That's the half-breed that was on the microphone!'

I turn and look in amazement as a pale white boy points and laughs at me. Behind him, to my disgust, is a group of jocks and cheerleaders holding a portable recorder. They mock my own words back at me as I glare at them.

'I know you didn't. I only just remembered. You may not be a jock and just a human,' says Hannah.

I almost lose my temper when I hear Marsha mocking my own words.

'My mother was slaughtered by the SOMMIT—by none other than my father! He's a member of the SOMMIT. What a joke, sistahs!'

Well, I will say, considering my temper and all, I'm impressed I don't pounce or rip them apart. Then I hear a familiar voice.

'You dearays leave ole Onyx alone, ya 'ear? She don' nothin' wrong to yew, so leave 'err be.'

'Oh, don't mind us, Doris. We superior ones just like to make sure vermin don't overrun our school.'

'Oh, Hannah, you got som' priorities to 'ort out 'n life. You can't go round sayin' tings like that about a perfectly good child! I oughta take you to yer parents to let them understand what you call people round 'ere!'

'Have I *offended* you here, Doris? How will I apologise?'

'That's enough, Hannah. Now I'm finished with your childish games, and frankly, Doris has come out here to serve you up some stew for the teacher–parent interviews this afternoon'

'What are you on about, you stray cat?'

''Ell, I can 'xplain that, 'Annah.'

To my excited eyes, Doris pours the large warm saucepan of stew right over Hannah's nice clean hair and uniform. Luckily, cheerleading uniforms go with anything—even embarrassment. Doris grabs me by the arm, and we run into the closest building. I'm between shocked, puzzled, and impressed with her actions just a moment ago. But something still bothers me. Why is she drastically leading me? Where is she leading me?

'Doris? What are you doing?'

'Gittin' you to understand somfin', Onyx.'

'What could that possibly be?'

''Our attitude 'bout who you are is quite atrocious, miss. You need ta learn who 'xactly ya are.'

'How will I do that? I don't exactly have parents to do that.'

'Ah, that just the ting', Onyx. There are those round 'ere that know a fair more than ya think.'

'Now you're making no sense, Doris.'

Suddenly, she stops. We are in the horticulture building, where the students have been caring for a miniature rainforest for over twelve years. We have been told once that the area that they look after is one acre—typical, as this used to all be farmland.

'Now, listen 'ere, Onyx. I'm goin' ta show you just what you 'av got yourself into. Your foot game friend, Jason, is alzo now involved. You are bof from different places but have been joined 'ere by fate.'

'What do you mean? I don't understand any of this.'

''Ell, let's just say you are not quite alon' in this 'ere world. There are more than you think.'

'What!'

'Look eva closa at these 'ere mushrooms, Onyx. Tell me what you see.'

I look close and hard at every defined detail of the small patch of mushrooms. One thing that's bizarre is that the mushrooms stand about ten centimetres high.

'I can't see anything out of the ordinary, Doris. What am I looking for?'

''Ell, let me show ye.'

Doris stands up tall after making sure no one was around. Quickly she gives a strange-patterned whistle. I watch the mushrooms and wait until the same whistle has replied. It sounds soft and small from the near distance. I look for the sound and discover a small purple light coming from behind one of the mushrooms.

'What is that, Doris?'

'That, deareh, is a forest pixie. Her name is Larvi. She is my sister.'

'Your sister is a forest pixie. Doris, that would mean—'

'Yes, Onyx, my sister and I are like you and your Aunt Jo.'

'Aunt Jo!'

'Oh, deareh, I'm guessin' she has not told you yet. Oh my, I do apologise. I guess I should let you know somefin'. Larvi, as you know, is a forest pixie from me dad side of the family, and I am human from me mom side. I am like me sister when it com' to mischief.'

'And what of your parents?'

''Ell, Mom died of old age, and forest pixies live longeh than humans, so dad is in the Amazon on holideh, lookin' for his grandfather, I tink.'

'So they are not with the SOMMIT?'

'Why no, deareh. We're not all been registered as being wot we are, if you git my drift.'

'Okay, and you were talking about Aunt Jo before. Is she really one of us?'

'Eh, 'ell, you see, Onyx, I didn't mean to say that, but I can tell you about how many there are out tare in the world. In this 'ere school alone, twenty are a lot like us. Your Principal Glosten has bat on her brother and mother's side. Sami too, he had bear, which is why he very hairy and has big veet. Good thing him Sami the slamming dunk basket ball guy, aye?'

'Principal Glosten! That explains why she understood so much.'

'Yes, Onyx, you be surprised who is out there—1 in 50 people 'av this gene within themselves.'

'Eh, 1 in 50! Oh my gosh, I thought it was 1 in 500! There are that many of us out there in the world? How do you know so much, Doris?'

'To be honest, Onyx, my grandmother endured what you are facing. The SOMMIT have dun cruel and nasty to us since the beginning, and she survived jus' like you, Onyx. She told us all about them, and we became aware since then.'

'That's incredible.'

'I don't men to be rude 'ere, Onyx, but I mus' get back to the tuck shop. Take care, and go speak with Aunt Jo. She be a wise woman, you know.'

'All right, Doris. Thank you.'

I can't believe the conversation that just occurred. Is all what Doris has said truthful, or is she just trying to comfort me? I look back at the mushrooms where

Larvi is staring curiously at me as she sits beautifully on a small mushroom. It takes me a while to figure what I should do or say. Firstly, I have never seen a forest pixie or one in a school forest; it's rather odd to me.

'Onyx, isn't it?'

My eyes widen for a moment, as I have the feeling she can hear my thoughts.

'Yeah, and you're Larvi, right?'

'Yes, yes, I am Larvi. I understand that you can be quite confused by all this, but it doesn't take long to discover yourself after discovering similarities with people around you. You may find yourself as if you're in a position where life is not that great, but what you haven't seen is the beauty in this world. Now go and take that first step of your life. Be glad you are only 17 and not 134 like me.'

She's 134 years of age . . . wow, she looks so much younger than that, though that could be the tininess of her.

'Larvi, um . . . uh . . . Never mind. I'll talk to you soon.'

On that note, I start to walk off until her little voice pierces my ears.

'Ask Jason one day who Demetri is. You may be surprised of what you'll find out.'

I turn and stare at the little being still calmly smiling on the mushroom. How does she know so much unless she speaks with people? Perhaps she can read people's thoughts. On that note though, who is Demetri? Many questions, yet so little time to get answers.

'By the way, Onyx, I can read thoughts, but only sometimes. It has to be a passionate subject, and you shall be surprised by what sort of things these kids have cooking in their brains. Take care, Onyx, and I hope you have an insightful afternoon.'

'See ya, Larvi.'

CHAPTER 9

Beginning to the End

With what was going on, surely after a day like today, this has to be a dream. In no more than one month, I have put two members of the SOMMIT in the hospital, ruined the south side of Franklin High, got a boyfriend, and found out that there are more uncaptured 'abominations' out there, living their lives the way they want. Perhaps I will have a chance to live my own life. I venture up to Principal Glosten and speak about the classroom Jason and I hang in.

'Principal Glosten, I was thinking of teaching gifted students about—well, you know—who are like me?'

'That's a good idea, Onyx. Well, you have the boards and materials. All you have to do is get the "gifted" students to come and learn.'

'But how?'

'That you'll have to figure out on your own, but I will sort out a select few that will certainly be interested.'

She smirks as if she already knows that this will be a successful idea.

'Ah, okay, thank you.'

'Any time. Take care, Onyx.'

After today being all it has been, I decide to skip my last class and head down to the shops to get a carton of milk. I then made my way back to the orphanage to speak with Aunt Jo.

'Oh, Onyx, you're home early.'

'Yeah, sorry about this, Aunt Jo. I guess it is just one of those days.'

'Hmm, well, I'm sure. Why, with all those jocks and cheerleaders making you busy, wouldn't be surprised if you haven't noticed everything else going on around you.'

'What do you mean by that, Aunt Jo?'

'Onyx, I think it is time that I tell you something. I've known about your abilities for a long time now—'

'I know. I have been here for a few months now.'

'No, no. Here, let me speak for a moment, as this is a bit difficult for me to say.'

She paused for a moment and directed me to follow her up the stairs, pausing in the hallway. Pulling down the stairway to the attic, we venture forth. In no time at all, my eyes adjust to the dark. As Aunt Jo lights a few lamps, I discover a whole room filled with folders and newspaper articles.

'What are we doing up here, Aunt Jo?'

'This is where I keep everything about our people, and in this folder is my family tree. Have a look.'

Smiling, she hands the folder to me. On the first page is a magical family tree background with multiple names scattered on it. Browsing through the names, I find my father, Michael Limestone, and joined to him are myself and a person named Lani Scarlett.

'Who is Lani Scarlett? And why am I on here?'

'Lani Scarlett is your mother, Onyx, and she is my sister.'

'Mother? Sister? That would mean that you are *actually* my Aunt Jo!'

'Yes, I am. I've been watching you for a long time.'

'How could you have been watching me, Aunt Jo? No offense, but you are a bit elderly.'

'Egyptian rulers in ancient times chose a family bloodline for each god. You are a descendant of Bastet, the cat goddess. I am from Horus, the bird god.'

That's why they said all those things years ago: 'This girl has the bloodline from the great cat demons, the one that has the family tree that dates back to ancient Egypt.' 'Wait, are you telling me that this child is a descendant of Egyptian rulers?'

'Onyx, even I don't understand everything from the ancient times. All I know is that the bloodline has been broken throughout the years, creating descendants and others like your friends Doris and Larvi. Only a select few are like you and me, containing the pure bloodline of ancient gods. We are slowly being dwindled. That is why you are such a prize to the SOMMIT. It has been 200 years since the SOMMIT has had a Bastet descendant, so they will stop at nothing to get you.'

'Two hundred years . . . I thought they were only a recent start-up.'

'No, they have been around for a great number of years. They did disappear for a long time. Their activities have only recently picked up, and their numbers have grown greatly.'

'I see—'

'Aunt Jo, I'm home!'

'Sinca! Time must have left us. I'm sorry, Onyx, but that is all I can really tell you at this time. You must find out the rest on your own.'

We leave the attic behind and prepare the orphans' afternoon tea and activities. I stay on the roof that night, my hair dancing in the wind, arguing with my shirt collar that beat against my neck and cat collar. The old one is wrapped around my boot to show where I came from, and my new custom one from Jason shows the changes I have undergone.

Off in a daze, I don't sense a nearby stray that joins me on the roof. We both stare at each other for a moment, curious about the differences between us. Are we that different? How much are we the same? I lie down on my back, looking at the faraway stars. The pure-black stray, as careless as they are, decides to keep warm by laying on my stomach. Eventually, we both doze off into a much-desired sleep.

The days go by, and the school is finally 100 per cent fixed. Principal Glosten and I have many meetings together, organising the classes that I will eventually be teaching. After putting together as much information as possible with the help of Doris and Aunt Jo, I have multiple topics ready to help the students. Principal Glosten still hasn't told me how many students have signed up. As Jason and I prepare our 'lectures', a bad gut feeling crosses over me. I can't shake off the feeling, and I know something bad is brewing.

'Are you all right?'

'Yeah, I just have a really bad gut feeling. I have this sudden urge to call the hospital.'

'Why?'

'The SOMMIT, I think they are moving again.'

'Onyx, why don't you give the hospital a call? If you have a bad feeling in your gut, it is always a good idea to follow it through.'

'Yeah, I guess you're right. I'll do that now.'

'Hi, thank you for calling Salem County Hospital. How may I be of service today?' said the receptionist.

'Hi, I'm calling about two men—Rohan and John. They were caught in an explosion just outside of town, and I just wanted to see how they were doing.'

'Let's see then. Rohan and John . . . ah, here we go. They were signed out last night by a practitioner named Charlie Benterson. Hello? Miss? Miss, are you there?'

I can't answer. The name rings through my ears and makes my heart race like a wild brumby. My eyes pause at the very wonder of why he's here.

Charlie, why are you here? Do you know where I have been after all these years?

I have so many questions that I know would have to be answered eventually. Jason grabs the phone and speaks with the receptionist. Slowly I can hear the sound of his voice as he puts his arm on my shoulder.

'Onyx, are you all right?'

'Uh, yes, yes, I'll be all right. Just a name I thought I'd never hear so close to home.'

'What was the name?'

'Charlie Benterson.'

'The SOMMIT.'

'Yes, very high in the ranks from last we met.'

'Yes, Dad has spoken about a Charlie before, though I didn't think he would be this close.'

'Me neither. I thought he was still in Transylvania, Louisiana.'

'Guess not. We'll get through it though.'

'We?'

'Yes, you don't think I'm going to leave your side, do you?'

'Well, I didn't really think about it.'

'Don't worry too much about it. Now come on, here're your books. Let's go teach our fellow students what it means to be different.'

'Yes, let's hope we have a few students on the other side of that door. Principal Glosten seems excited, I hope we can help them.'

'We will. Now come on, or we'll be late.' He smiles so confidently at me as if saying 'Congratulations, we will tackle and solve the problem together and get through it as one team.' It has been a long and hard battle to start the 'creature club', as it was still commonly known from Hannah and Marsha. But I guess those two will never change. At least they make life slightly amusing and challenging with their juvenile actions.

In the classroom, I'm about to attempt to teach my variety of students about themselves. Thanks to my new friends, that sounds amazing to say. There are genuine friends in my life—Doris, Larvi, and Jason. They will learn a lot, I hope, and will have more opportunities with our combined knowledge than what I've had. My aim is to teach them how to protect themselves and learn how to identify the SOMMIT. Principal Glosten will be keeping a sharp eye out in the community to make sure that the SOMMIT will not interfere with the students and families of Franklin High.

Jason walks up to me with a smile. 'You ready, Onyx?'

I look down at the books that I'm holding. The top one ironically is titled *The SOMMIT.* All hand written notes collected through the years. A little piece of all our history is contained in these books. For each of us to learn and hopefully, live a life where we can be all of who we are.

'We're not out of this just yet, are we, Jason?'

'No, but we'll all be all right.'

Epilogue

It hasn't been easy, but the school is finally starting to accept differences in people as well as Onyx.

Next Book in the Series

The High School Girl: Investigation Realisation

Onyx has been taken. Charlie makes his debut appearance with a mysterious woman with glowing green eyes. This time, Onyx realises that she is not alone. There are others that she needs to consider in the decisions she makes.

A green luminescent injection in the possession of the SOMMIT raises alarming questions. What is the SOMMIT planning?

Gut instinct will not be enough this time. Onyx has to admit that even she needs help in returning to Salem to uncover the answers to her questions.

More of her history is uncovered along her travels, and strange interactions question how truthful those around her are. Who can be trusted, and who is lying for their own agenda?

Printed in the United States
By Bookmasters